A Play's the Thing

written and illustrated by **Aliki**

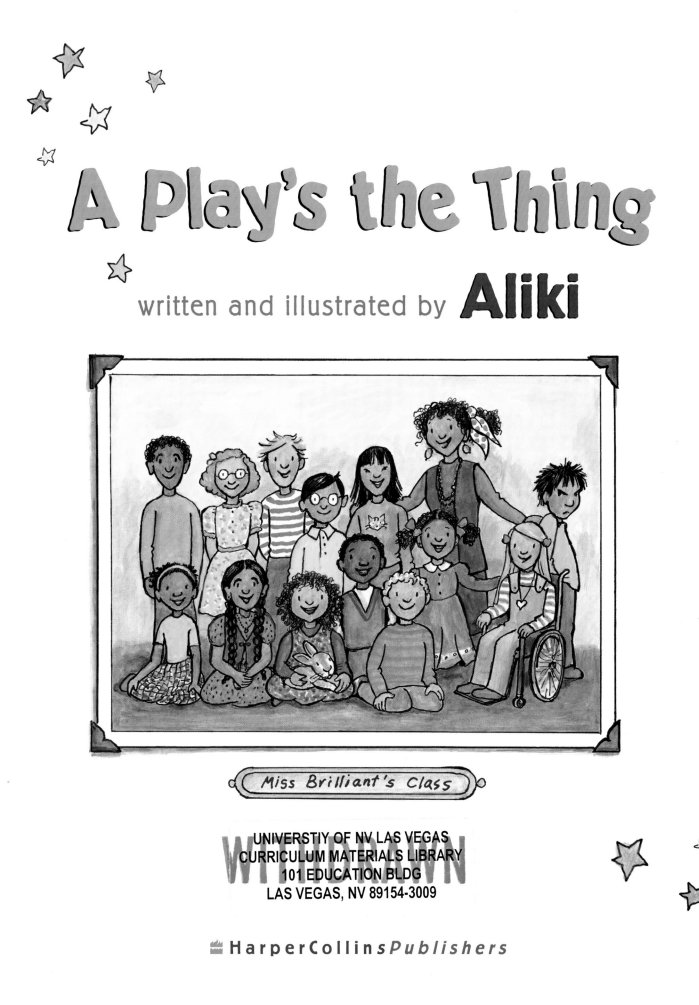

Miss Brilliant's Class

HarperCollins*Publishers*

Library of Congress Cataloging-in-Publication Data

Aliki.   A play's the thing / by Aliki.–1st ed.   p.   cm.

Summary: Miss Brilliant's class puts on a performance of "Mary had a little lamb."

ISBN 0-06-074355-7 – ISBN 0-06-074356-5 (lib. bdg.)

[1. Schools–Fiction. 2. Theater–Fiction. 3. Nursery rhymes–Fiction.]

I. Title: Play is the thing. II. Title.

PZ7.A397Pl 2005   2004022101   [E]–dc22   CIP   AC

Typography by Martha Rago

1 2 3 4 5 6 7 8 9 10 ❖ First Edition

This book is for

Bill Morris,

the best of the best.

And to all those who breathed life

into Miss Brilliant and her class.

This is Miss Brilliant.

This is Miss Brilliant's class.

There's Yashi, Carmen, Ricardo and Steffi, Miyoko, Igor, and Cameron.

There's Sophia, Willa, Abdullah, Hannah, Bandana. And there is José.

Miss Brilliant is full of ideas.

She likes to celebrate.
She celebrates everything.

Teeth.

Corn.

Mummies.

Spiders.

2 Monday Afternoon

Miss Brilliant collects the test papers.

"Now let's celebrate," she says.
"We'll put on a play!"

"We will do *Mary Had a Little Lamb*," says Miss Brilliant.

"We'll write more parts," says Miss Brilliant.

"We'll add the tension," says Miss Brilliant.
"We'll add the fun."

"We will all get to sing," says Miss Brilliant.

"We'll do it next Friday," says Miss Brilliant.
"Now turn to page 22 in *Poetry Please*."

Miss Brilliant announces the cast.

Carmen will be Mary.

Yashi will be the lamb.

Hannah will be the dog.

Miyoko will be the cat.

Willa will be the firefighter.

Cameron will be the Bully.

José will be the teacher.

"We are a team," says Miss Brilliant.
"Everyone will get a part.
We will all work on the script.
We will cooperate and have fun.
But now it is time for math."

In between science,

social studies,

math,

tests,

and homework,

the class cooks up a storm.

They all get parts.

They study their scripts.

They memorize their words.

They practice.

They cut,   paste,   paint,

collect,

and write out invitations.

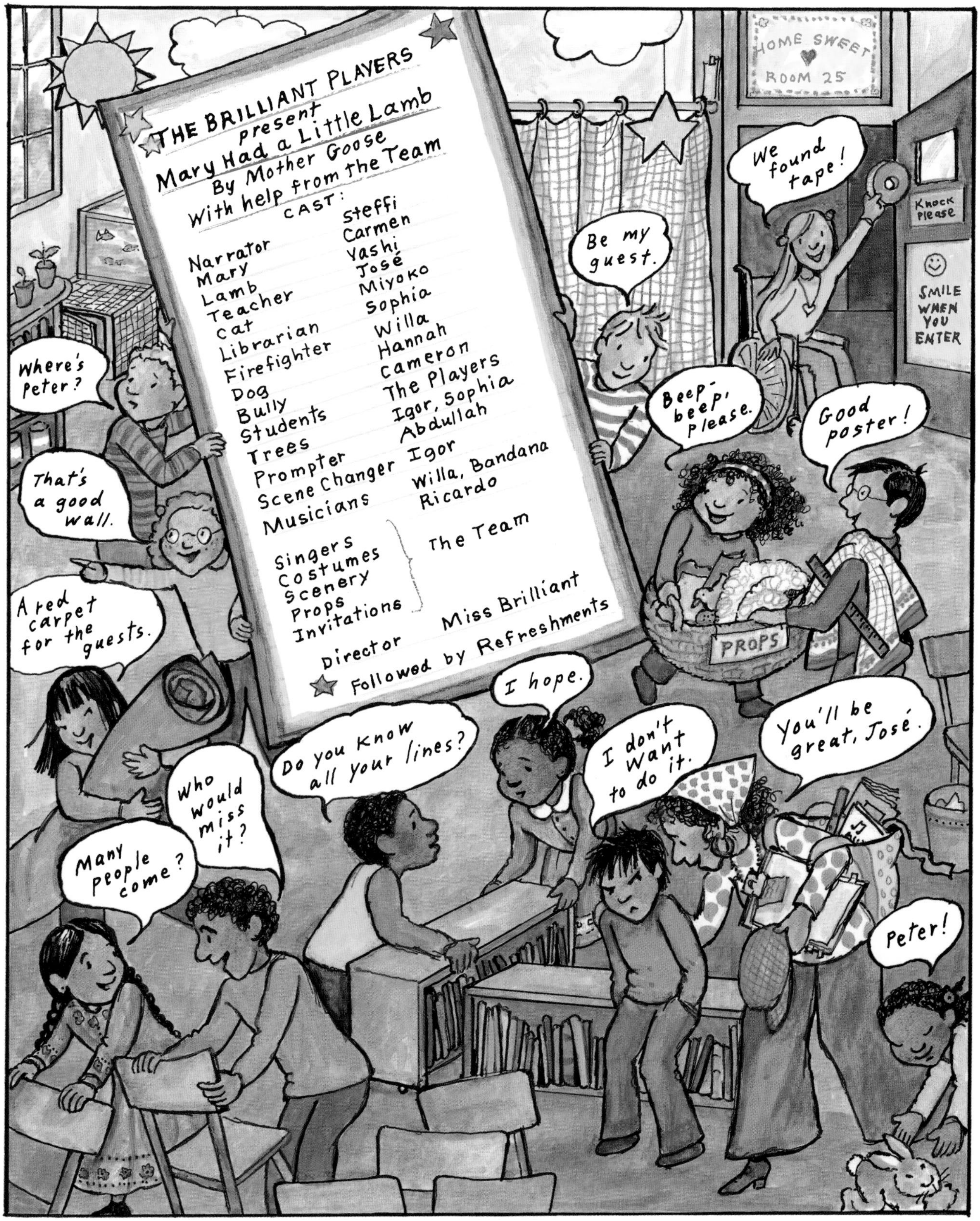

By Friday, they are ready.

6 The Big Day

Family and friends crowd in.

Ding, ding.

"Good luck, Team," says Miss Brilliant.

Curtain!

7 The Play

ACT ONE . . .

Mary had a little lamb,

Its fleece was white as snow.

And everywhere that Mary went,

The lamb was sure to go.

It followed her to school one day,

That was against the rule.

It made the children laugh

and play

To see a lamb at school.

And so the teacher turned it out,

But still it lingered near,

And waited patiently about

Till Mary did appear.

Why does the lamb love Mary so?

The eager children cry.

Why, Mary loves the lamb, you know,

The teacher did reply.

The audience claps.

Cameras flash.

The players bow.

They celebrate.

Everyone is proud.

9 End of the Day

The class is jubilant.

Miss Brilliant is too.

They laugh.

They congratulate each other

and share ideas of their own.

Then Miss Brilliant pops the last idea of the day.

José's heart thumps.

His mind races.

He hears voices.

José gathers his courage.

He makes his decision.

The class cheers.

"Time to go," says Miss Brilliant.

"Your fans are waiting!"

What a way to end the day.